We got nothing left. All I hope for is a tie.

A one-in-a-thousand freak thing happens. The puck ski-jumps right over my left shoulder, hits the underside of the crossbar, and dives straight into the net.

I look up at the clock while their team mobs the kid. Three stinking seconds left. That's all we had to use up for a tie.

They stop celebrating, win the face-off at center. The buzzer sounds. I skate to the gate in the boards and hammer on the glass with my stick to be let out. Behind me Coach Cooper is hollering for me to come and line up and go through the handshake deal, but a guy opens the gate for me and I head for the locker room.

I have absolutely no interest in pretending to be a good loser. Believe me: There is no such thing.

ZIP

Other Novels by Bruce Brooks

Asylum for Nightface

What Hearts

Everywhere

No Kidding

Midnight Hour Encores

The Moves Make the Man

THE WOLFBAY WINGS

Woodsie

Cody

ZIP

BRUCE BROOKS

A LAURA GERINGER BOOK

HarperTrophy®
A Division of HarperCollinsPublishers

Zip

Copyright © 1997 by Bruce Brooks

Library of Congress Cataloging-in-Publication Data
Brooks, Bruce.
    Zip / by Bruce Brooks.
        p.   cm. — (The Wolfbay Wings ; #2)
    "A Laura Geringer book."
    Summary: Ten-year-old Zip struggles to deal with his best
friend's defection to a rival hockey team, a move that will test
their friendship and leave them face to face on opposite sides
in a close game.
    ISBN 0-06-440598-2 (pbk.) — ISBN 0-06-027350-X (lib.
bdg.)
    [1. Hockey—Fiction. 2. Friendship—Fiction.] I. Title.
II. Series: Brooks, Bruce. Wolfbay Wings ; #2.
PZ7.B7913Zi   1997   97-2049
[Fic]—dc21   CIP
                                                  AC

Typography by Steve Scott
1 2 3 4 5 6 7 8 9 10
❖
First Edition

Visit us on the World Wide Web!
http://www.harperchildrens.com

*To Ryan, Randy, Colin, Chris, Moose,
Nate, 'Nother Colin, Kyle, Brian, Andrew,
Brendan, Mickey, Robbie, Matt, Jason,
Brooksie, and, above all, to Eric Lewis.*

ZIP

'm reading one of my brother's big-deal collectible Sandman books and bending back the cover because I am a mean little jerk when I hear Kenny Moseby holler up for me from the yard. Moseby used to come to the front door and knock, being a very polite boy, but one time my mother answered the door, told him she would get me, and on her way to get me heard something blow up in the kitchen, which she went to fix in kind of a panic. She forgot about leaving Moze on the doormat. It is typical of Moze that he just stood there waiting, wouldn't knock again, for almost half an hour. Since then he comes around beneath my window and hollers, "Hey, Zip."

Used to be six or seven times a day. But he hasn't been around for about a month now.

I don't bother to get up. "Get poked," I yell, hoping I sound bored.

"Hey, Zip," he repeats, as if he hadn't just said it.

"Get reamed."

"Hey, Zip."

"Get tooled."

And so on. Finally I run out of verbs. Verbs are the only words I like; I have a lot of them. I go to the window and look down.

Moseby's standing there flat-footed, hands at his sides, looking up flat-faced. I open the window and spit, making sure I miss, but not by much.

"Sorry, Moze," I say. "I have a puck in my throat and it makes me kind of hawk a lot. I'll probably have it surgically removed after the season if it doesn't get dislodged by another one between now and then."

He swallows, and says, "I heard it was bad."

"It wasn't *bad*," I say. "And I heard you had four goals in two games and six assists in another."

He kind of nods, looking away from my eyes.

"Now *that's* bad," I say. "*That* sucks."

"Listen, Zip—"

"In fact, I think *you* suck, Moze, so good-bye." I try to slam the window down, but wooden windows don't really slam in late October.

I go back to the graphic novel and bend the cover worse. Too bad for my brother. It isn't *his* fault my best friend left my hockey club and went off and scored like 41 goals in three games for the enemy while my team lost three games by a margin of like 236 goals, all but 17 scored on me. I guess there is no justice.

A minute later Moseby walks into my room.

"I just opened the door," he explains, very guilty.

"That's what one does with doors," I say. "Congratulations." I keep reading.

He sprawls on Scott's bed. Nobody says dip. Then he kind of casually says, "So how does Scott like Bantams?"

"He says they will never lose which means he will never play, so Bantams are unpleasant too in their own special way. But not of course like Squirts. And not like me. I *play*."

"I'm sorry you got hammered," he says.

"No problem, Mozer."

He nods as if he believes me. Which of course makes me madder, so after another minute I throw the book across the room. The spine hits the wall hard, just below Scott's Joe Juneau poster; the sharp noise sounds a little like a puck snapping onto a stick blade, and that makes Moseby's antennae twitch. His mouth's probably watering too. Moseby's entire mind and body drops everything at any stimulus that suggests hockey action.

I used to really like this about him—in fact, I was in awe of it, though most of the time I mocked him. It was one of the reasons we were pals. I like hockey all right, but I am not in love with it. I never hustle in practice, I gripe about skating drills, I goof off, I never concentrate except during games. When I don't hustle, people accept it because I am a goalie and taking it slack is a goalie thing. But it's just that I don't give a puck sometimes. Every week or so I think about quitting, and the idea never really hurts. I keep playing, but usually not by much of a margin. It's just easier to play than to stop. My dad would flip. Since I started playing hockey he has become a vice president of the Wolfbay club, and he is one of the co-managers of the rink, and my mom's friends are all hockey moms now, and it's a complete family lifestyle. It wasn't that way when Scott was the only one playing. They thought

Scott was just weird to take up this bizarre ice game. When the Baby started, it became a family deal. Now they all like it a lot more than I do.

Moseby is not like me. Moseby cannot remember his childhood before he started skating at age five. He doesn't care about those years—who needs to remember a time when you liked fire trucks? Life started with hockey. Listen, Moze doesn't sleep but about three hours a night. He lies there twitching with the awful feeling that, somewhere, someone is skating with a puck *without him*, and this drives him nuts. Moseby will quit hockey when the undertaker peels his cold, dead fingers from his stick. Once when he had the flu, he thought he was going to die and he called me to issue his final request: He wanted to be buried in his skates *without the blade guards* and he wanted to make certain he was dressed in his *road* uniform, because he always liked it better.

Of course he is the greatest player there is. Not just around here, either—last year he kicked the butts of all the teams from Boston, Minnesota, wherever. Everything from his skating to his shot shows he lives for this, everything shows he has found his joy in life. I think it's sick, but what the heck, maybe I'd be the same if I were that good. I think about that a lot: Is Moze great because he loves it so much, or does he love it so much because he's so good? Because when you're as good as he is, there's more to it than practice. When you're that good, it's because of some extra, weird thing inside.

Since he left the Wings, I hate all this hockey-love stuff in him. All of it strikes me as sick for sure. I wish he'd wake up one day and realize he only cared about girls or chess or some other crap. He sucks.

"So what are you doing here?" I ask, as the Sandman book slides down the wall. "Couldn't resist rubbing it in?"

He turns red, and I feel a little bad for saying something I know isn't even possibly true but which I also know he would treat like it could be. "No, man, jeez, I—"

"What number are you this year, Moze? Still 22?"

He looks puzzled. "I wasn't 22 on the Wings. I was 28. And I'm still 28."

I yawn. "Thought it was 22. Never mind."

That gets him. He turns white. I yawn again. Across the room he droops his head into his hands. I smile.

If I was going to get beat 22–4 on the Wings, and Moze was going to get six goals in a 14–1 victory for Montrose, then he could stand some pain. And I could give it to him.

I smile for a long time.

two

People say: You have to hate yourself a little bit to be a goalie. That's a crock.

Basically, see, a goaltender's job is just the opposite of what normal guys go through life trying to do, which is, get *out* of the way of things people try to *hit* you with. See, everyone has this need to believe life is a series of attacks which, through toughness and sweaty glorious full-color courage, you somehow live through. Very dramatic, very gritty, makes you feel like a "survivor" and all that stuff. But the story for a goalie is different: For us, people are trying very hard *not* to hit us, but we insist on getting in their way.

The classic goalie profile, at least in Canada, where kids play hockey all the time on the frozen pond in the backyard from age seven months on, probably wrapping diapers around their legs for pads and using rulers for sticks, is that the goalie is always the weakest or fattest or slowest kid who can't stand up for himself and is therefore bullied into playing the inferior position.

But that isn't the way it is here in the U.S., at least outside of the northern states like Minnesota and North Dakota that are practically part of Canada anyway. Down here, the kids who play ice hockey have to do it in rinks, and to get on the ice they have to be on organized teams, with uniforms and slick equipment and coaches and Zambonis and the whole deal, and it all requires commitment and money and probably a lot of hours of watching the NHL on the Deuce. To these kids, playing goalie is like the *coolest.*

I don't say this just because I am a goalie and therefore I must be cool, although this happens to be true. I say it because that is how kids feel: A lot of people want to play goal and be the star and the save-your-team's-butt go-to guy and wear a cool painted mask and get rubbed on the head after every game and all that mess. If you are the goalie, you get to act weird and funny and mean, you get to scowl and mutter to yourself and snap at people, even at adults; you get to laugh crazily in the middle of games and bark like a dog if you want, you get to hit guys with your stick pretty regularly, you get to do almost anything, and even the referees just go, "Well—that's what goalies are like."

Getting away with almost anything is pretty frosty. But eventually you have to go out on the ice and keep some pucks out of the net, or else you look like you totally suck, in front of absolutely everybody, and your teammates hate you and their parents criticize you and your coach sighs because you are the only kid who owns leg pads and therefore he has to play you and feels cursed. This is the time when most goalie prospects decide to move up to winger.

Well, good-bye to all those suckers; hope you score a *bunch* o' goals, dudes! I happen to be excellent at keeping the puck out of the net, so I have always remained a goalie. And though I go to every goaltender clinic you can imagine, and learn from former semipro goalies all about the mechanics of the inner-edge slide-step and the vectors of shots and the angles of cutdown and the use of the knees, the fact is, I am one hundred percent what they call a reflex goalie. You shoot the puck at me and I stop it, somehow. I don't plan, I don't see you coming and think, "Jeez, this looks like an obtuse-angle low shot that, given the ice conditions this morning, is likely to topple instead of saucer, so I had best get my blocker tilted at twenty degrees and shift my weight to the outside edge of my left skate and cut down the angle by sixty degrees . . ."

Forget that crap. You shoot, I react, the puck stays out of the net (most of the time). It's simple. And it requires absolutely no homework.

Let me put it this way: If you shot the puck ten times exactly the same way from the same spot, I would stop you nine times, and each save would look completely different. But a study-goalie, a book-goalie, would stop you exactly the same way each time: His body would look like a photograph of his previous save.

But he would only get you eight times. Because something happens a little different on each shot. You can either go by the book or by the puck, and frankly, nobody has shot a book at me yet.

Every goalie will say that a bad team can lose games for a good goalie, and that a bad goalie can lose games for a good team. Both things are true.

But I never met a goalie who believed he really was bad. So every time he got popped, he thought it was the defense's fault, not his own.

Me too. This weekend I gave up almost forty goals. Trying hard to be fair, I can admit that I let in five that I should maybe have stopped. The rest came from bad play in front of me, because my team is made up of clods and losers.

I hate getting beat. I do not play to "play." I don't buy all the crap about sports being a process and you have to enjoy the process, never mind the end result. That's not me. I put up with the whole game so I can be a winner at the end, and sneer at the losers. I put up with the hassle of following the puck as it zips around through legs and skates and sticks, I put up with flopping onto the ice, I put up with the ugly thick stuff I hang on my body, just so I can catch a puck and show it in my glove to the frustrated buttmunch who shot it and laugh in his face. I am not a nice boy. I do not like nice boys.

I used to like one, though. Kenny Moseby is the nicest boy there is. Or he was until he left me.

know the puck is behind me in the net, but I don't bother to turn around and fish it out. Dooby does. He doesn't look at me, but he says something.

"Hey, Zip, like maybe if you could try to give a crap?"

"Kiss my cup, Doobs."

He flips the puck up to Jerry Cooper, Jr., the goody-goody Bantam superstar who helps his dad run practices. Jerry whizzes to center ice for a face-off, stopping all flashy with one of his famous sprays. All the little Squirt Wingsies say "Ooh!" and look at him with admiring eyes.

Dooby is still hanging around. "You can't pretend you don't care. Letting in weak shots doesn't hide the fact that you can't stop some hard ones even if you try."

"Why don't you try to get a couple past me,

Doober?" I laugh. "The only 'hard one' you ever get ahold of—"

"Hey, that's really clever, Zip," he says, back-skating away. "Wiener jokes. Very dignified. No doubt very *goalie*." He spins and sets for the face-off.

Twenty seconds later a medium-fast shot from the point goes over my shoulder.

"Nice shot, Woodsie," says Coach Cooper.

"It was not a nice shot," I shout. "It *reeked*, like all Woodsie's shots. He ought to do nothing but pass."

"Why didn't you stop it, then?" Coach asks coolly.

"Because I reek too. See, I *have* to reek, because I want to feel I belong on this team. I'm looking for that common bond with my brothers in ice."

"Grow up," says Barry. "We've only lost four games."

"By an average margin of thirteen goals," I add.

"And of course the goaltender has no responsibility for that," says Boot.

"Haven't seen *you* notching the ol' hat tricks, Mr. Offense."

Coach blows his whistle back at center ice. "Face off," he says.

"That's what we're doing," I snap.

He's bent over, holding the puck above the crossed sticks of Cody and Prince, but he looks down the ice at me. "It's not time for that yet," he says. He holds my eye. "Do you understand, Zip?"

I scrape some ice from my crease, skate side to side a couple of times. I look back up. He's waiting. Everyone is.

"All right," I say. "But how long do I have to wait? How many games do we lose before I can throw myself completely into a sulk? It's going to be hard to stop."

"Try stopping a few more pucks first," he says. "That seems to be hard enough." He drops the puck. Prince wins. The action moves down to Marshall's end. Ernie sails a shot from the high slot. Marshall saves it, stops the rebound shot from Prince, dives on the puck, comes up rattling it in his glove. He looks down the ice at me and tosses the puck.

"Nice save," says Coach Cooper.

"No kidding," Marshall says loudly.

always frown and cuss and
crank at everyone before games.
I don't always feel all that cranky, but it *is*
a goalie thing, certainly a Zip thing by now, and
everyone expects it. So, just for *fun*, before our next
game I am cheerful and sweet. I offer Ernie some
tape; he gawps at me and stretches out a nervous
hand. I put my arm around Woodsie, who is always
wound very tight, and tell him to cut loose and
have *faith* in those incredibly creative passes he
always wants to make. He looks at me like I'm
somebody's nerdy dad. It's great. I tell Boot he
needs to shoot the puck more. He frowns and says,
"Well, of *course*," and shakes his head.

During warm-ups I keep telling the guys to
shoot high. If they get one past me I say, "Good
snap on that one, Mario!" Usually, of course, I for-
bid high stuff and chop the ankles of anyone who
lifts it; also I cuss out anyone whose shot I don't

save. At the pregame buzzer when I skate to the bench for the scrum around the Coach, I interrupt his moderately optimistic pep talk by hooting and saying, "Let's cut their droopies off, teammates!" Coach just looks at me, then names the starting line. I swat everyone I can reach on the butt and skate back to my cage. When the ref looks up for my signal that I'm ready for the face-off, I holler, "Drop it, Ralph! Behind my defense, I am fearful only of not seeing enough rubber!"

Prince wins the face-off, pulling it back to Dooby, but their left wing intercepts his pass, skates around Woodsie, draws Doobs while his center jumps in for a two-on-one, and slides it across to the center for a tap-in past my right skate.

"My fault," says Dooby, fishing the puck out. "No, *my* fault," says Woodsie, skating up to tap my pads tentatively.

"Hey, teammates." I grin through my face cage. "Enough of this guilt stuff! We're all brothers!"

By the end of the first period I have made eleven incredible saves, flashing out kicks, whipping the glove, even one time taking a slapper off the chest, falling onto my back as the puck toppled over my face toward the goal, but swatting it into the seats with my stick at the last second. However, thanks to rebounds that go uncleared, odd-man rushes including one three-on-none, and a couple of superb tips from centers who no one bothered to clear from in front of me, we are down 7–0.

"Want a rest, Zip?" asks Coach Coop as I skate up to the bench. Marshall, I notice, is not on the bench. That means he is in the locker room changing from his terrible-right-wing equipment to his even-worse-goalie equipment.

"No way," I say, and veer off toward the other cage. "We can *take* these chumps."

After the second period we are down 11–1. Woodsie makes a nice pass across the ice to Cody for a one-on-one and a nice goal for our nice team, just to keep it respectable. Coach sits me for the third. Marshall lets in eight in the last period. Boot, who never gives up in his personal quest for glory, scores two. Final: 19–3.

"Almost had 'em, dudes," I say, as soon as we are all in the locker room.

"What is it, Zip?" Barry asks. "You have something *real* to say?"

"Just that he misses his bestest pal," says Dooby, yanking off a skate.

"What I miss is hockey."

"Aw, do you like hockey, Zippy?"

"The real game?"

"The graceful swoops of the speeding wingers, the bone-jarring—it's always bone-jarring, right?— checks of the gritty defensemen, the gymnastic flips of the keenly focused goaltenders? The thwack of a puck going tape to tape, the swish of skates gliding over smooth ice, the curse of disappointment as the goalie robs a zipping forward flicking a precision pass top-shelf? Is that what you miss, poor ol' Zip? In all of its elegant purity?"

"Frankly, yes."

Dooby yanks off his other skate. "Then go get a picture of Eric Lindros and take it to bed with you and your hockey stick."

"Or a picture of Kenny Moseby," says Ernie.

I stand up, take Dooby's skate from his hand, walk over to Ernie, and take his chin in my hand. He gapes, much as he did when I offered him the tape before the game. Smiling down at him, I lightly move the skate blade across his forehead. A very thin line of blood appears, a trickle starts. As I leave I know it won't be bad. On the head, cuts always look worse than they are.

hile all the phone calls ring back and forth above my head in the house, I play my drums in the basement. I can pretty much anticipate the calls and count them off as they come: protests from Ernie's parents, calls from my mom to Coach Cooper and back to Ernie's parents to verify that the "wound" was no big deal and required no official medical attention, a call to Ernie himself that I have to make so I can apologize officially. "Sorry, Ernie," I say. "It's okay, Zip," he says. Then he pauses and adds, "I shouldn't have said that about Kenny." I say, "Yeah, maybe not, but I shouldn't have listened," and that's it.

Drums are not what you think. You don't beat your frustrations out on them, because in fact drums throw everything right back at you. Pop a tom-tom with a stick and before you are even aware you have struck the skin, the stick is back where it started, poised above the drum. The only difference is there's a little *poom* in the air somewhere. You don't just smack 'em the way everyone thinks, with them just sitting there taking all the abuse without fighting back. Nothing does that. I remember my science class: There is always an equal and opposite reaction.

The basement door opens after a while and Cody comes in with his guitar slung over his back and his little amp in both hands. Some snow comes in with him. He shivers as he butts the door closed.

"Your dad bring you in this?"

"Walked."

"What a Canadian." Around here, the slightest dust of snow—especially this early in the year—causes grown-ups to shut down their lives and huddle around piles of canned food as if nuclear bombs were only minutes away from falling.

Cody drops his amp near an outlet and un-slings his guitar. "Two entire inches are anticipated. I may be spending the next few nights. My mom wouldn't want me to risk wandering into a drift by walking the four blocks home."

Without saying much more, we set up to play. I hadn't known he would be coming over—nobody ever knows Cody's coming over; he just shows up with some kind of equipment that sets what you're going to be doing for the next couple of hours—but since I'm down here anyway, it's fine. I go get out the floor tom-tom that's going to be one of my Christmas presents and I'm not supposed to *really* know about or use until then. Cody plugs everything in and splangs a sick chord. It isn't nearly loud enough, so he turns his amp up.

He looks at me behind my drums. I nod. He considers his left hand on the guitar neck for a moment, then screws his fingers into some bizarre shape and whams the strings with his right. It sounds great, like a car wreck. I smash a cymbal and hit both tom-toms hard and then cut into a fast *smack-boom-smack-boom* beat with my snare and bass. Cody wails away. Once in a while we play in the same rhythm for a few seconds and Cody nods, but then we move on. After about ten minutes he stops. I do a pretty lousy roll from snare to tom to floor tom and hit both my cymbals.

"What do you think?" he asks.

"Let's call it 'A Leaf Falling.'"

He nods. Then we do it all again at a slightly slower tempo, me trying out a kind of fake reggae beat a few times, Cody getting into some slashing power chords in the same rhythm and actually at one point playing a few lines on a single string. We end after six or seven minutes.

"'The Kiss,'" Cody suggests.

"'The First Kiss,'" I say. He nods.

"I wish I could get some lessons," he says. "I need to learn how to do feedback and stuff."

"You need a big amp for that, I think."

"This thing is for babies to play Beatles songs on."

"Let's play a Beatles song."

"Okay," he says. "Which one?"

I shrug. "Do you remember any titles?"

"I think there was one called 'Holding Your Hand' or some crap like that."

"Right," I say, tapping my sticks together. "'Holding Your Hand,' from the top, in C minor. One, two, one, two . . ." Then we make eight more minutes of ugly noise.

"How about a little Beethoven now?"

"Can't," says Cody, frowning at his guitar, from which a curly wire dangles. "I broke a string. It's the highest one, too."

"Cool. Let's see if you can break a couple more."

"Nah," he says. "And I don't know how to put a new one on." He starts stowing the guitar away.

"Why not keep playing, Codes? I mean, does it make much difference? Do you, like . . ." Here I lift my chin and put on a fake British accent. ". . . feel that your full chordal eloquence will be inhibited by the removal of one sixth of your melodic reper-toire or something?"

He shrugs. "Something like that." He zips his case. "It will sound like *worse* crap without that string. And I guess it's okay for us to suck on pur-pose, but I don't want to suck when the sucking is out of my control because I'm, like, missing some-thing."

He looks at me. I put my drumsticks down. He doesn't need to say it but he does. "Maybe kind of like the way you feel about the team now that we're missing Kenny and the other guys."

"Yeah," I say. "Okay. And look what you're doing—you're quitting too."

With his hands in his pockets he looks at his zipped-up case. "Yeah. But there's two differences. One, I can get my brother to put a string on, and I'll be back tomorrow ready to go. And, two, I can't really do anything *but* suck. I mean, it's fun to bash the guitar and hear you bash the drums, but neither of us knows doo-doo about really playing." He looks at me, shrugs again.

"But you mean we *do* know how to play hockey beneath the sucking."

"You're a great goalie, Zip. And you love to stop guys and make them feel crappy. And you even like some of us, some of your teammates, or at least you used to. Kenny wasn't your *only* friend or anything."

I pick up a stick and swat the tom-tom. *Poom.* "Yeah, but Kenny was my only friend who could score a hundred goals." Cody just looks at me. "And Joseph was the only defenseman who could clear every rebound," I continue. "And Justin was the only other defenseman who knew how to watch guys in the slot so they didn't get point-blank shots at me whenever they wanted. And . . ."

"It's not that," Cody says. He starts to put on his coat. "I don't believe it's all just hockey stuff. It's not just 'skills,'" he kind of sneers. He wraps a red scarf around his neck and slings his guitar case onto his back. "It's that you don't think you're good enough to save a bad team."

"Nobody is," I say.

"Then maybe no team is really bad." He shrugs again, which makes his guitar jump. Then he leaves and shuts the door.

I stay where I am and do some really sucky rolls for a while. Then I quit and go upstairs and play on the computer for an hour or so. I have just beaten the evil three-headed Gwamcha, Guardian of the Eighth Level where the Red Diamonds stolen from the Kingdom of Natima may be hidden, when I realize I did not restore the Santa Claus Surprise floor tom-tom to its hiding place. If my mother goes downstairs and sees that I have been using it . . . Oh well. So what. Santa will just have to come early this year.

six

Scott shovels a spoonful of Kix into his mouth and doesn't bother to chew before saying, "The Montrose Squirts are awesome."

My father looks up from the sports section and glances at me before asking, "You saw them?"

Scott gulps, shovels, crunches once. "They were playing Northern Virginia in the slot before ours in Reston last night. I watched most of the third period." Scott too looks at me. "Kenny played awesome."

"Well, that's just *awesome*," I say, taking a bite of toast.

"What was the score?" my father asks.

"You know what the score was already," I say. "You don't go to bed before you know how every league game ended. Don't try to get all tricky and softhearted, or I'll puke right into Scott's bowl of little round crunches of pure corn flavor."

"Okay." My father sighs heavily. "The score was 13–2."

"How many did Kenny get?"

"At least three," Scott says. He isn't eating his cereal anymore. "I saw that many. Plus a couple nice defensive plays hustling back when Wayne Bellis pinched, which he always does too much."

"Wayne Bellis sucks as a defenseman," I say. "He screens his goalie with his big butt and always tries to stickhandle the puck away from guys in the slot instead of just knocking them onto their pants. The only reason he's on an A team is that he has a good shot from the point."

"He scored two," Scott mutters.

"And I'm sure Cheerios was marvelous," I say. "You don't have to hide that from me either. Cheerios is a good goalie. He plays angles better than anybody. He stands up great. I can't believe he stays up the way he does. He says it's natural, but I think it's some kind of weird willpower. When the puck is sliding around in front of you, you just go *down*. You don't intend to. You just find yourself with your pads spread on—"

"If Mason hadn't chosen to play elsewhere this

year, do you think you'd be starting every game?" my father asks calmly. He's the only person in the whole Wolfbay club that always uses kids' real names. Even Cheerios's mother calls him Cheerios. Same with Boot.

I know my dad's trying to find something good about those jerks betraying us. I also know he was more furious than anybody when they made their decisions, and tried every way he could to prevent them from jumping clubs, taking the cases all the way to the commissioner of the Capital Beltway Hockey League. See, you sign these sort of contract things when you start with a club. But it turns out you can get out of them if you notify your club by a certain date before the season starts.

But I don't want him to find something good. "What that really means is that because 'Mason chose to play elsewhere,' I get to be blasted every minute with no relief. Do I like to play hockey? Sure. Would I hate sitting on the bench all the time? You bet. But do I appreciate being humiliated every game? Figure it out."

"What I think you don't appreciate the most," my father says, snapping his newspaper back, "is being left behind by your friends."

"It's not that they were my friends," I say. "It's that they were my team."

"Well," says Scott, with beautiful timing, "they sure play great with their new team. Montrose is going to rule."

Later in the afternoon my mom calls me to the phone. It's Kenny Moseby.

"Hey, man," he says, all cheery.

"Congrats on the big win," I say.

"Thanks. It wasn't exactly a big win, though. Our guys kind of dominated, like, and, you know . . ."

"Yeah, I heard the score. Must be tough never finding anyone who can challenge you and all."

I was sneering but he took it straight. "Well, I hear White Lake and Lancaster are both pretty good," he says. "We go to PA in two weeks and play both of them. Ought to be fun."

"Yeah, and in the meantime it's just ho-hum, kick butt."

"Zip, I can't help it we're good. This team had a lot of awesome players even before, you know—"

"Yeah, but why bother joining them, then?

What's the point? Especially since we both know those 'awesome' Montrose stars are all a bunch of noseholes. We used to *hate* those guys, always talking trash and giving us cheap stick fouls behind the play, all changing into their team warm-up suits and primping around the rink together for two hours after every game and the parents with the color-coordinated pom-poms and the bumper stickers that say MY KID KICKS ICE AT MONTROSE HOCKEY CLUB."

He says softly, "Some of them aren't so bad once you get to know them."

"You mean, once you're no longer on the receiving end of their chops behind the knee. Sure. But have you thought, have you even thought, about what you're going to feel like when you play us and somebody like Jeff Moore or Archie Pelletier spears Doobs or cross-checks Cody in the back of the neck?"

Even more softly he says, "Of course I've thought about it."

"Hey, maybe you'll even have to, like, pass some new-boy test, you know? Come out for your first shift against us and give your old buddy Prince a two-handed slash, just to prove to your new teammates where your true loyalty lies."

He's quiet for a long time. Then he says, "Zip, I need you to keep being my friend."

"Don't make me puke," I say. "Is that why you called?"

"No," he says, recovering some of his voice. "I saw on the schedule you guys play Northern Virginia next and I thought maybe I'd tell you a couple things I noticed about some of their shooters."

"Jeez, that's thoughtful. Offer some tips about a team you beat 13–2. Because obviously we need all the help we can get."

For a second he gets mad. Kenny never gets mad. "Well, okay, yes! So what's so bad about that? You guys *aren't* likely to dominate, are you? What am I supposed to do, pretend I haven't noticed you're getting your tails kicked? This isn't a very competitive team, okay? So you guys might not be overmatched. You might have a chance to actually beat them, right? So, you want the tips, Zip, or you want to lose proudly all on your own?"

I swallow a few times. He breathes hard. Finally I say, "I'll take the tips."

enny was at least partly right about Northern Virginia's Squirt A's: They don't jump all over us and make it clear after three shifts that we ought to quit. Their players skate better than ours in general, but they are not especially creative and their timing is off, two things that mean their coach doesn't know how to get the best out of them. Which is fine with me. After the third offside whistle ruining the third three-on-two coming at me, I begin to relax and think maybe we'll have some fun today.

It's true they spend most of the first half-period in our end. But their plays are set and predictable, which means even our guys can start intercepting their passes and clearing the puck to center. And when their forwards do shoot at me, they aren't sneaky about it, so I see the puck all the way and knock it aside with a laugh. They have one player—a guy Kenny said he could only tell me to watch out for because he was pretty awesome—who fools me on a backhand and scores, but I stop three other guys on partial breakaways (it takes our defensemen a while to warm up) entirely because they do things Kenny told me they would, like looking down at the puck if they're going to lift it instead of looking at me if they're shooting it on the ice, and stuff like that. Kenny watches everything.

After their star beats me for the first goal, though, something unusual happens, which is that we manage to get the puck down into their end and keep it there for a few passes. And I have to admit, we *do* have some creative players. At one point Prince fakes a shot from the circle and blindly backhands it up the slot to Woodsie, who was creeping in, and then Woodsie winds up for a slapshot just long enough to give the goalie a chance to slide desperately over to stop his slapper, but instead Woodsie turns his stick blade at the last second of his downstroke and snaps it on the ice right back to Prince, who has snuck up to the far post, and *he* taps it in. On the next shift Cody and Boot work a give-and-go from the back boards and Boot scores and we are actually leading, for the first time all year.

It goes to our heads right away, because Barry immediately lets a guy get past him for a clean break-away. I slide out, set my stick across my skates, hold my glove ready, and scream *"Come on, nosehole!"* as I always like to do. He dekes to the backhand but I only pretend to go for it, because almost nobody goes straight to the backhand and shoots on a breakaway, and then he tries to snap it forehand into the top cor-ner, but I whip my glove up and catch it. He skeets to a stop and smacks the ice with his stick to show he knows he blew it, so I skate over and hold my glove under his eyes and flop it open to show the puck. "Lookee!" I say. "You popped up to the second base-man!"

"That's enough," the ref says, and I toss him the puck, and Ernie and Shinny and Woodsie skate by and smack my pads. "Just tell Barry to kiss my bleep," I snarl at them. Off the face-off, Woodsie, who is the team's best passer and always moves the puck with his head up, scanning the ice like the last thing he wants to do is carry it himself and is looking desperately to get rid of it but then all of a sudden you notice he's crossing the other blue line with a sudden burst of semi-speed and bearing down on the goalie, does just that, and *does* go straight to his backhand and scores. 3–1. Not too bad. The period ends.

Early in the second, Cody half-fans on a shot from the circle and the goalie goes down as if it were coming full speed, sliding out just far enough so that it trickles past him. I feel sorry for the poor sucker but not *too* sorry. Especially after their star guy skates right between three of our players and whips a wrist shot that I don't even see under my blocker. 4–2. Then for about ten minutes there's a lot of skating and passing and intercepting in the neutral zone, but no more shots on either goal except a long ridiculous softy from almost the red line by one of their wingers, which I skate out and take on my forehand and fire back at him twice as hard, hollering "Try again, fool." Second period ends.

At the break, everyone's excited, maybe *too* excited, jabbering, "We *got* these guys! These guys *suck*!" and all that crap. I can tell Coach Cooper is having trouble deciding whether to let the enthusiasm carry over in the hope that it will turn into confidence instead of foolishness, or to get stern and bring everyone down and make us focus on playing conservative, defensive hockey. He watches everybody for a few seconds and it's like I can read his mind: *Let 'em have their fun*, he thinks to himself, and he smiles and joins in the whole let's-stay-pumped thing, and my heart sinks. I want to play it safe. The hell with fun. Let's just win this sucker.

The third period starts and we go right at them, and on the first shift Boot scores a pretty goal on another incredible no-look pass from Woodsie and I think, Well, maybe Coach is right. Then we get it right back into their zone and we're whipping passes all over the place and the defensemen are getting into it and Woodsie decides to cheat up and get another assist, but he coughs up the puck to a winger charging him and the kid has a clean breakaway and he beats me. Two shifts later the same thing happens to Ernie when he pinches in to keep the puck along the boards in the zone but misses it, and I stop the breakaway with a kick save but nobody picks up the center trailing the play and he taps in the rebound. Suddenly it's a one-goal game, and suddenly *they* are skating and *we* are tired. The puck starts hanging around in our zone now, and our guys can't seem to remember how to defend even the predictable offense, and before you know it the center is standing at one post completely uncovered with the puck, and the right wing is standing completely uncovered on the other edge of the crease, and I decide to slide both pads at the post in the hope of stopping either the shot or the pass. But the pass gets by and the wing ties the game and our defensemen are still looking around for someone to cover.

To our credit we rally a little and put on a flurry, but now their goalie is excited and he stops Cody on a point-blank with his pads and then snatches Shinny's rebound shot out of the air with a shout. And that's it for us; we got nothing left. All I hope for is a tie.

Just a freaking tie. I look at the clock. There are only twenty-one seconds left. Face-off down there. A scramble. Puck behind the net. Another scramble. I look up: down to twelve seconds.

But then one of their defensemen digs the puck out and snaps a clear pass to the star guy, who is streaking full speed up the right wing. I see the defenseman on that side, Dooby, is turned the wrong way and the guy is past him in a heartbeat. But as I look across the ice I see Woodsie, good old conservative Woodsie, who always anticipates the worst, hustling back from the other point, skating like a wild man to catch the star with the puck. *"Check his ass!"* I scream. Watching them skate, I can see just the path the star is hoping to take to me, and just the path Woodsie is hoping to take to cut him off, as if there were dotted lines painted on the ice. They close in. The star is faster, but he's carrying the puck close, which slows him a little, and Woodsie can hustle like nobody, and suddenly it's clear that the dotted lines are going to intersect—Woodsie *is* going to cut him off. So the star pulls his stick back to get off a clear shot even if it's a worse angle and farther out than he wanted, and Woodsie does exactly the right thing, which is lunge and jab his stick blade out in front of the puck to make it ski-jump way up, probably over the glass, harmless. But a one-in-a-thousand freak thing happens and his stick blade is angled too low and instead of ski-jumping over the glass the puck ski-jumps right over my left shoulder, and hits the underside of the crossbar, and dives straight into the net.

I look up at the clock while their team mobs the kid and Woodsie hangs his head. Three stinking seconds left. That's all we had to use up for a tie. Three seconds.

They stop celebrating, win the face-off at center, the buzzer sounds, and I skate to the gate in the boards and hammer on the glass with my stick to be let out. Behind me Woodsie is trying to apologize and Coach Cooper is hollering for me to come and line up and go through the handshake deal, but a guy opens the gate for me and I head for the locker room. Marshall can shake everybody's hand twice and that will have to do for the Great Brotherhood of Goalies.

I have absolutely no interest in pretending to be a good loser. Believe me: There is no such thing.

'm playing my drums along with one of my dad's old surf-guitar records turned up real loud, when the basement door opens and I expect to see Cody again. But it's Kenny.

I finish pounding out a tom-tom roll at the end of a song called "Banzai Pipeline." Kenny waits till it's over and says, "Hi."

I grin at him. "Wow, hi, Ken! You're just in time for 'Slaughter on Tenth Avenue'!" Then I start smacking my snare and hi-hat, completely out of rhythm.

Unfortunately, "Slaughter on Tenth Avenue" is the last song on this side of my dad's record, so I either have to get up and walk over to the turntable and flip it and walk back and take my seat again, which will provide many moments for talking, or I can stay here and pop the drums, thus perhaps making enough noise to prevent any talk. I decide to do that, but Kenny—always considerate, every parent's favorite child—goes and flips the record for me himself and doesn't say a word. Suddenly I don't want to play along anymore. I put down my sticks.

"Did you do the math homework yet?" he asks.

"Yes," I lie. "The answer is 'Two.'"

"Ah," he says, nodding, embarrassed at my meanness.

"Suck my nose, Moze," I say, climbing down from behind the drums. "You didn't come over here to talk about homework."

He frowns. "How do *you* know?"

I get a grape soda from the basement fridge and don't offer him one. "Because the only math you're interested in is the addition of assists to goals, creating a sum that defines who you are, in your splendid entirety."

"You know that's not true."

"You're right," I say, burping. "It's not. I hasten to add that your mathematical interest is broader: You also count team wins and losses."

He sighs, leans against the wall with his hands in his pockets. I burp a couple more times. After a minute he looks up and says, all serious and meaningful, "How much longer are you going to treat me like this, Zip? I mean it."

"As long as you're sucker enough to keep coming around and taking it."

He frowns again; I can tell it's hard for him to say what he's about to say. "We've been best friends since before kindergarten. You *like* me. I'm not a different person just because I wear a Montrose jersey three times a week."

"You're right again," I say. I walk over to him and stick my face close to his. He just watches me with his large blue eyes. "You're absolutely right. But, see, Ken, *I'm* a different person just because you wear a Montrose jersey three times a week."

Then I burp, right in his face, and turn and go upstairs. He doesn't follow. The song that's playing is "Walk, Don't Run." I don't hear him close the basement door. He never slams doors.

have to give Coach Coop credit. While his team keeps losing games by dozens of goals, in what should have been total flaming humiliation, to jeering goons who not only outscore us but knock us on our butts whenever they want to, he manages to keep everybody but me pretty happy. In the locker room before games, everybody jokes and jabbers all excited, just as if we're about to go play a meaningful role in a hockey game. Then, back in the same room an hour later, just after we've been outskated, outstrategized, outshot, outdefended, and *should* have been out*raged*, all the Li'l Guys sulk for no more than thirty seconds and then start whooping it up as if we had actually been playing out there, instead of being toyed with. A couple of the more intense players take longer to recover—Barry, Dooby, and Woodsie, who's the worst and always cries, sobbing like in fury for a couple of minutes with his glove over his face so everyone can pretend we don't hear him—but after a while everyone is just hootchy-koo, throwing tape balls and laughing and stuff. Some of the goody-goody dads make sure to go around the whole room and say Something Encouraging to Each Child, but otherwise no mention is made of the nuclear annihilation we've just undergone. Coach Coop tells us when the next practice is and leaves. The guys split in chummy groups of three or four, wearing their Wings jackets, hanging out, being tight.

The practices are just a great old time for everybody (but me) too. I don't know how Cody and Doobs and Boot and Prince and Barry and the other old-timey Wings stand it, but Coach very patiently tries to teach the new guys fundamentals of hockey *we* all learned when we were six. But Cody and Doobs are right in there, joining in drills about How to Follow a Shot for a Rebound just like the idea was brand-new and brilliant. This is the Squirt A's, and half of them have to be taught where to stand on the breakout! That's first-year rec-league stuff! It's ridiculous. It's insulting. One time I said so to Dooby when he asked me why I was sulking.

"What's insulting about learning to play hockey?" he said.

"Supposedly we already *know* how to play hockey, dumb-ass. I mean, is this a travel team, or what? An A travel team? Do you think the Montrose A's spend all their ice time inching along pushing pucks around cones with the idea being not to look down too, too much to see if the little rascal has scooted off your stick? Sheez. We're taking two weeks going over the amazing concept of a centering pass while they're practicing six variations on a ten-pass rotation scheme for the power play."

Dooby shrugged. "Good for them. They ought to win theirselfs a *big* ol' mess o' games."

"But—"

"But this is *this* team. And even though we probably won't win a single game, this is *our* team, Mr. Bigtime. And some of these idiots *don't* know what a centering pass is, and so we'll all go over it until they do." He leaned close to my face cage. "Because we're a *team*, dumb-ass. A team that is *terrible* at playing hockey, but is actually getting to be pretty decent at being a *team.*" He shoved me in the chest. "You're welcome to join, any time, or at least until Marshall gets decent enough to play in your place." Then he skated away.

The next Saturday we play two teams from north of Philly. I lose the first one 7–2. Marshall loses the second 16–6 (a weaker team, obviously, when you look at our stunning goal total; even Ernie scored). After the first game, Coach asks if I want to dress out for the second and play a little wing. I say no. I watch the game from the bench, dressed in my goalie stuff. I guess I think acting like a contented backup is kind of a courtesy to Marshall, who sits in his pads and watches me most of the time. He stinks, and even scored one goal on himself when he tries to deflect a pass coming through the crease.

But afterwards, when we're shuffling through the handshake line, he turns to me and says, "In case you're feeling like a bigshot, you know, at least 16–6 is a lot better ratio than 7–2."

"Well, then, let me be the first to congratulate you, Marsh-Man," I say. "And may I add that I'm very impressed you know the word 'ratio,' even though it has absolutely no application to goalie statistics."

"I know the word 'ratio' too," says Dooby, who's behind us. We look at him. He has taken off his helmet and steam is rising from his scalp. Sweat trickles down his face like tears. His eyes look as lifeless as nickels. "'Ratio' is Spanish for 'Bite my tail, Marshall, if you think you have anything to celebrate.' Or maybe you're happy about netting that goal, which *does* tie you for fourth in the team scoring race."

Marshall ducks his head and turns back to his handshaking. In the locker room afterwards, I gave him the nickname Sniper. I'm afraid it sticks. I couldn't resist. Nobody else could either. I can tell how bad it hurt him when everybody starts jiving with it. But by the time we're dressed, he's starting to play along, saying he's going to get a goalie stick with a little more shooter's curve to it, promising to score his next one on the backhand. I confess it kind of blows me away that he manages to get happy and jive along with the guys. Marshall is usually a real redbutt, always shouting out blame at other players, noticing whenever they mess up, complaining. The thought crosses my mind that maybe Doobs was right. Maybe this *is* a "team." A team that even an obvious jerk like Marshall can belong to.

ten

I used to spend pretty much all my time after school and on weekends with Kenny. We didn't do that much, just hung out. It was one of those kind of automatic things. We never invited each other over, or said, "Hey, what are you doing Saturday before practice?" It was always just, like, well, here we are doing whatever it is together. When we talked about stuff, I was always the sarcastic cranky guy and Kenny was the nice guy, but these were just sort of the roles we took. I never *really* thought I was that much of a mean jerk. But since blowing Kenny off, I have become even more of the person I used to kind of just *act* like for fun, knowing Kenny was there to sweeten things up. Oh well.

In the months since I started blowing Kenny off, nobody has, like, emerged in his place. I mean, I haven't really made a new friend, or promoted an old semi-friend. Cody comes over, but

Cody's pretty much his own guy. Woodsie invited me to spend a Friday night at his house once when his older sister was away and it would just be us and his dad, who is not a bad guy as dads go. I actually wanted to do it, but I said no. I don't know why. Later I heard he got Barry to come, and they watched three PG-13 movies, sent out for pizza *twice*, and, *with* Woodsie's dad, had a Wiffle Ball tournament in the living room with all of the furniture shoved against the wall, until they broke a window at around 2 A.M. The next day they all went to the hardware store and bought a big sheet of glass and came home and Mr. Woods taught them how to cut it and then how to take out the busted pane and put it in, which sounds pretty cool actually. Cutting glass.

So what I'm saying is, I suppose I'm lonely. It's a nerdy word, I know, and it kills me to say it. It's a nerdy *concept*. But it's the only way to explain some things I find myself doing. One of the strangest is that I have actually begun starting conversations with my brother. Scott is an okay guy, I mean he's not one of those big brothers who beat you up all the time and mock you when you get interested in stuff he's already outgrown and all that. The trouble with Scott is that he is incredibly boring. He plays hockey, he collects comic books, he has a buddy named Allen and a girlfriend named Melody whose hand he holds every possible second of the day. These are the only things Scott thinks about, and the big problem is that he is incapable of thinking or talking about them with any humor. He is the only person I have ever met who has never said a single funny thing. Even my father, who is not exactly the Laugh King himself, seems like Jim Carrey compared to ol' Scottie.

Talking to a boring person seems like it should at least be a pretty safe way to waste time, but there is actually a certain danger in it. People who aren't especially quick to pick up the subtleties can ignorantly drag you into blunt discussions of things other people know better than to talk about. For example, one day when Scott and I were lying on our beds reading comics he just asked, "How come Kenny never comes over?"

I squirmed a little, and said, "Jeez, Scott, get a brain. I mean, you know." I looked over at him. His face was blank.

"What?" he said.

"Well, I don't know. I mean, it's pretty obvious, isn't it? He quit the Wings. He went to Montrose. He left. He's gone."

Scott continued to look mildly blank. "So? Doesn't he still live two blocks away? Don't you still go to the same school?"

I closed my comic and kind of slapped it onto the bed. "Yeah, but so what? Moving to the Montrose A's is like moving to Russia. He's a traitor. He's just *gone*."

Scott blinked. "It's just hockey, Zip. He's got a chance to play for a coach who played in the NHL, with a bunch of guys who are almost as good as he is. It's a nice opportunity."

"Yeah," I said, "well, I hope he has a 'nice' time." I opened my comic again and pretended to read. Out of the corner of my eye I could see Scott's face still turned toward me.

"But it's not just hockey to you, I guess," he said.

I slammed down the comic. "What's that sup-posed to mean? I hope you're not getting ready to say something like a guidance counselor."

"You think he betrayed *you*. You think he

should have passed up the chance to play for Marco because you guys are buddies."

"*Were* buddies."

"Whatever." He blinked some more. "Look, Kenny loves hockey."

"No kidding. More, obviously, than he likes people."

"No, that's not true. But why should he hold himself back from going as far as he can with the thing he loves?"

"No reason at all. Provided you don't mind chucking the best friend you ever had."

Scott frowned. "Is that what you think he did? 'Chucked' you? On purpose? Just by changing hockey teams?"

"Of course." I noticed with alarm that I was suddenly choking up.

Scott watched me and shook his head. "Did it ever occur to you that maybe Kenny had no idea he would lose your friendship?"

"What—"

"Did it ever occur to you that maybe Kenny thought you guys were good enough friends that you would understand? That maybe you'd even be happy for him? And that for sure something like playing a year for another club wouldn't threaten something as solid as being best friends with you? Ever think of it that way?"

"No," I said. "And nobody with any sense would think of it that way either."

Scott raised his comic and started reading again. "Kenny's got plenty of sense," he said.

I was scowling and about to leak, so I turned onto my side with my back to Scott. "Sense, maybe. But what he doesn't have is loyalty."

Scott didn't say anything for a minute. Then, just as I was calming down, he spoke again. "Maybe he's not the one who's missing some loyalty," he said. "He changed his hockey jersey. You sound like *you* changed your heart."

"Only some dweeb who holds hands with a girl would talk about 'heart,'" I said. "Don't make me barf."

"All right," he said. "I won't. But maybe instead of barfing you should do some thinking."

"I'd rather barf."

"Then get my comic out of the way, will you? That one's worth six dollars. Thanks."

eleven

On Saturday we have a very early game (which we lose 14–2, bringing our record to 0–8–0) and nothing else until a game against Bethesda at 9 P.M. I bang the drums for a while, watch the fish swim around my mother's aquarium (it's salt water and you practically can't breathe within ten feet of it because you might screw up the salinity balance or the alkalinity balance or something and cause immediate death to all of these fish that cost more than Yankee outfielders, but I like to watch them and take the bold risk anyway). Then Mom and Scott come back from his morning game (won 6–0) and Dad returns from a Wolfbay Board meeting and suddenly I have to get outside. So I put on my Rollerblades and hit the streets.

No hockey stick, no ball, no pads. No direction. Just wheels, a tailwind that seems to stick with me as I go around corners, and good speed. I keep to the street getting up a good sweat. It's weird, but the kind of sweating I do during games in goal is different from the kind you get from plain old exercise. Goalies don't move much. We have to be great skaters, so we can maneuver in a very small area, but we never skate long enough to make us sweat a drop. Instead of exertion, what we have is tension. It's not that tension you get from being scared or nervous—for me, it's a clean sort of tightness that comes from concentrating.

Nobody concentrates like a goalie. I heard at one of my hockey camps last summer that there's a new theory, telling you to make yourself look away from the puck once in a while (when it's down in the other end, I guess) and think about the beach, or your girlfriend, or whatever gives you some kind of mental refreshment, which allows you to concentrate in a more "natural cycle of attention" or something. Forget it. There is not supposed to be *anything* natural about playing goal. And most of the people I know tell you never to let up for a second. If the puck is down in the other end being passed between two of your own players, keep your eye on it—

because it's the same puck that might hit a stick and disappear behind some skates and end up some-where you didn't see it get to, and then four of the bad guys are coming at you full speed, spread across the red line, and you have to scan to see which of them is carrying the puck and by that time one of them is probably shooting it at you from an angle you have not covered and then you are bathed in the lovely scarlet glow of the goal light.

So concentrate, when you're in the cage, and sweat. Think about the beach in math class.

I unzip my jacket halfway and the cold air bil-lows it out. My nice-relaxed-exercise sweat starts to chill me just right. I pivot and skate half a block backwards, right down the middle of the street, getting a little tickle-thrill from the risk of not being able to see where I'm going. I pivot back to frontways at the corner, and almost slam into Coach Cooper's van, which is stopped smack in the middle of the road, idling.

"What say, Zipper?" the Coach calls, leaning out his window. Cody looks across from the other side of the front seat and gives me a nod.

"Not much," I pant.

"Saving some of that energy for the game tonight?"

"Sure. Am I playing?"

"You're the one."

"Get this, Zip," Cody says. "Marshall's dressing *out*. He wants to play a little *center*, he says. He went and bought two aluminum-shaft sticks!"

"The Sniper!"

"Got hisself some of that bad goal fever!"

"He'll never put the pads on again."

"That poster of Eddie Belfour in his bedroom? It's *down*, Jack—bet on it. Boy's put up a Brett freaking Hull."

I frown seriously. "This forces me to perform an unpleasant duty. The fact is, even the *intention* of playing offense gets him kicked out of the Great Brotherhood of Goalies, effective immediately."

"Hey, get in the van," Cody says.

"Where are you going?"

Coach says, "To Reston. To scout the Reston A's. We play them next Sunday. I've never seen them."

"And to stop by the Tower Records in the mall just down from the rink. I'm getting the new Red Hot Chili Peppers CD."

"Hop in," Coach says. "We'll swing by and pick up your shoes."

I hold up my hand. "Wait a minute. We're going to drive for an hour, to go watch some kids play hockey? *We* have already played one game, we have another one in a few hours, and in between we're going to watch people we don't even know do the same thing? That's sick."

"It's at the new Reston rink," Coach says. "I haven't seen it yet, either."

"A pitiful excuse."

But I get in, we grab my shoes, and off we go. In about two blocks Cody starts begging to stop and get some food, so we pull into a 7-Eleven and Coach lets Cody buy two full-size bags of chips and two packs of cupcakes and three hot dogs and a few drinks and a couple of candy bars. "To share," Cody explains.

"That's very generous of you, Cody," says his father as he forks over about twelve dollars.

We get back in the van and drive and eat and talk, mostly about all the cusswords Cody has heard are featured on the new Red Hot Chili Peppers CD. At one point I turn to his dad and ask,

"You approve of this?"

He shrugs. "So far he hasn't mentioned a term he won't hear frequently at any hockey rink."

We get to northern Virginia and drive past about thirty malls. When we turn into the rink parking lot the coach drives once all the way around the building, studying it and grunting now and then.

"Isn't it kind of big?" says Cody.

"There are two rinks inside," Coach says. "Both Olympic."

"Then I'm glad we play these guys at home," I say. "I get too tired playing on big ice."

They both laugh. We get out, go through a nice carpeted lobby with *two* snack bars and a very fancy-looking hockey shop. "Nobody but rich yuppies lives out here," Cody says. "Their daddies all buy them a hundred-dollar pro jersey after every victory, just as a little 'positive reinforcement.'"

"Your dad spends that every week on cheese puffs for you, so what's the difference?" I say.

Coach has been looking around. "The Squirts are on the rink over there. We can go down to the ice, or we can watch from that room up those stairs, which is apparently some kind of comfortable place to sit and observe the yuppie children at play." He doesn't sound like he thinks very highly of the room.

But Cody does. "A luxury box!" he says, running for the stairs. "Cool!"

He's almost right. It's a large carpeted room full of pretty nice (non-folding) padded chairs, with restrooms down a hallway off to one side and two televisions in the back corners, where some little brothers and sisters are watching cartoons. The front wall of the room is a huge sheet of glass, with the rink right down below. Parents are gathered around, chairs placed carefully so they don't block each other's view.

"Think there's a bar?" says Cody. "I could use a margarita, just to get me in that nice, calm, hockey-watching mood."

Coach has already found some seats among the parents, most of whom turn and check us out and smile and nod. Almost all of the men are wearing corduroys and nice sweaters and some of the women actually have dresses on. But not the small woman standing at the corner of the glass. She's wearing very old jeans and hightop basketball shoes and a black sweatshirt. With a shiver I realize that she is familiar, and then a second later who she is.

Just then she turns and sees us. She smiles hugely at me. "Well, Zip!"

It's Kenny Moseby's mom.

"You didn't tell me they were playing Montrose," I say to the Coach and Cody. "You didn't—how could you even come?"

Mrs. Moseby has walked over and she puts her hands on my shoulders. I look at her. She's smiling, and it is a very nice smile, one that I have known since I was about three. Probably seen it ten thousand times. I try to look away, but I can't. "Hi," I finally manage to say.

"It's nice to see you," she says quietly, and gives my shoulders a light squeeze. Then she lets her arms down and says, "Would you like to stand and watch with me, or do you prefer to sit with your lazy coach and his no-account son?"

Coach Cooper laughs. "I can't help noticing you're closer to the heating vent over there, Marie."

"Well, Jerry, I've gotten soft and pampered."

"Oh, I'm sure they're taking care of you. How's

that new house in Ocean City they bought you so Kenny would jump?"

"They promised beachfront, but it's bayside," she says. "So we're considering coming back if the Wings have a better offer."

I can't believe these two people are even speaking to each other, much less joking in a nice friendly way, even less about Kenny's disgusting treachery. Even Cody cracks a joke. What the hell's going on?

Suddenly there's the sound of a buzzer, muffled by the glass, and Mrs. Moseby hurries back to her spot. Cody motions me to come and sit next to him, but I cut him cold. I find a place to stand by myself.

Sure enough, down on the ice I see skaters in the familiar blue-and-yellow road uniforms of the Montrose Bears, lining up across from kids in white uniforms with bright-blue trim. My chest burns as I spot the incredibly familiar form leaning into hockey position at left wing, slightly bow-legged, left hand a little too low on the stick, head very slightly tilted to the right, looking like he's watching the puck in the ref's hand and seeing a lot more there than any other kid on the ice does. Kenny Kenny Kenny. In blue and yellow.

The ref drops the puck. The centers stab at it, and, sure enough, before it seems anyone else can quite bring himself to move, Kenny Moseby has darted between them and kicked the puck ahead and taken it on his forehand and deked around one defenseman scurrying to catch him and then cut severely back to the high slot as the other defense-man whizzes by, making a perfect screen between Kenny and the goaltender, who never even sees Kenny's low backhander until it is behind him in the string.

"Kenny," I say.

On the ice most of the kids in white are kind of standing around like "surely the game hasn't *really* started yet, right?" and the Montrose kids are coolly lining up for another face-off at center, Kenny already there in his bowlegged stoop, looking like he'd never moved. Up in the luxury observation deck, the Reston parents are all just as confused, looking at each other as if to say, "Did somebody just do something?" The scoreboard says RESTON 0— VISITORS 1. The only people who get it are the four of us, Cody and Coach and Mrs. Moze and me, because we have seen it hundreds of times. But in different colors.

Another face-off. The Montrose center wins, pulling it back to the left defenseman, and I am certain he's going to bang it off the boards around the Reston right wing to Kenny sneaking fast toward the blue line, because that's what *we* always would have done—you just always found Kenny and let him take care of things. But instead, this kid looks that way, fakes the pass, then megs the center with an incredibly perfect saucer pass that the Montrose right wing takes just over the blue line, coming in fast. Both defensemen go to him and Kenny is open, so of course I know he's going to pass it to K, but instead this winger makes an impossible cut with an impossible pop of speed right between the defenders, beats Kenny to the net by eight feet, and casually whips a backhander top shelf that knocks the goalie's water bottle three feet in the air.

Whoa.

Coach Marco leaves the same line on, even though it seems like they've played enough for three shifts—but when I look at the clock I see only thirty-one seconds have ticked away. This time Reston wins the draw (the parents in the luxury box cheer weakly) and put together a nice three-man rush that catches the Montrose center in a pivot and turns into a three-on-two. The Reston center makes a nice blind pass just right to the left wing, but the Montrose defenseman times a poke check perfectly and pops the puck away. But the center has swung behind his pass and he one-times the puck past the other Montrose defender to his right wing, who is all alone at the right edge of the crease and *he* one-times it perfectly. But somehow Cheerios has slid across with his pads stacked and the shot thuds. It's an incredible save. Unfortunately, the puck has taken a soft rebound and is just sitting smack between the pipes, just ripe for a tap-in, as Cheerios squirms on his back. I smile. I've been there. The Reston center jabs his stick at the puck.

But cool as can be, a Montrose defenseman lifts the center's stick and skates through it, picking the puck off the line, leaping two-footed over Cheerios without missing a beat, blowing by the Reston right wing, and firing a pass up to Kenny, who has circled over the red line so he can take it onside going full speed. He beats the lone defenseman with a casual fake, comes straight in on the goalie, draws his stick back, the goalie drops into just the right spot, and Kenny spreads his skates and taps a backhand pass backwards. The Montrose center is there for it in the high slot just as if they'd drawn this up on a blackboard, and he rips a shot. Unfortunately it hits the far post and ricochets in front of the goalie so he can fall on it and stop this madness for a minute.

I look up at the clock as the lines change. The game is one minute forty-two seconds old and it ought to be 3–0 already.

No defenseman on our team would have cleared the rebound the way that Montrose guy did. No center on our team would have trailed Kenny so perfectly and ripped that shot. And frankly, I don't think I would have come close to making that save Cheerios did.

Hmm.

The second line comes out and dominates just as bad, running plays at full speed as if the Reston kids weren't there, playing just perfect hockey. A couple of the kids who left the Wings with Kenny are in that unit. They fire at least six excellent shots on the Reston goalie, who is actually superb, stopping all but one of them. The third line comes out, and plays the same way. They score two, the last one on a three-man give-and-go with a pick, a play our guys—even our guys last year—could not have understood in a half hour of diagramming, much less been able to do. And this is the third line.

Mrs. Moze is at my shoulder. As if she's reading my thoughts, she says softly, "Marco really is quite the coach."

I just shake my head. Everyone in the room is silent.

At the end of the first period the score is 10–0 and it is obvious Marco has told the guys to take it a little easy. They make unnecessary passes, rag the puck, practice their stickhandling, shoot it soft. When the buzzer sounds, Coach Cooper stands up. He looks at me and raises his eyebrows. "Ready to go?"

I start to leave but there's a hand on my arm, so I turn. Mrs. Moze looks at me as if she understands everything, including the things I don't. "You're welcome to stay and ride back with Kenny and me," she says.

I look down and shake my head.

She doesn't take her hand off my arm. Finally I look up at her again. "We miss you," she says. "Kenny misses you."

I kind of snort. "Yeah, well, we miss him. Seen our record?"

"I'm not talking about hockey," she says. "You know what I mean."

I nod my head toward the ice. "With *that* kind of hockey, what else do you need?"

I stare at her kind of arrogant. She just looks into my eyes, and smiles slightly. Finally she takes her hand off my arm and says, "Yes, well. It *is* good to see you. And we would love to see more of you. Please come by the house anytime. As you used to."

I move away. "I'm pretty busy stopping pucks. But thanks anyway."

In the car on the way back, Coach Cooper is silent, looking thoughtful, no doubt exercising a commendable adult carefulness in This Delicate Situation. Cody, however, yaps without pause, about the Montrose A's. Did I see that drop pass by

Number 18? Could I believe the way that defense-man, Number 6 or 9 or maybe it was both, could shoot from the point? Low and hard and right on net—jeez. What about Number 10 and Number 32—could they stickhandle, or what?

Finally he pauses, and shakes his head incredulously. "I guess the thing that's so awesome," he says, "is that, like, Kenny's just one of the *guys* on that team. He's not, like, you know, the *man*. He just *fits in*. It's weird, isn't it? I mean, you'd think a kid would rather stay somewhere he was a star instead of finding a place where he was just normal."

I want to say: If you knew Kenny like I do, that wouldn't surprise you at all. If you knew Kenny like I do, you'd understand. If you knew Kenny like I do . . . But I don't say anything at all, because I wonder why all of a sudden I know that I know so much about Kenny.

couting Reston didn't do us much good. Maybe they were mad about being destroyed by our neighbors from Montrose. Maybe their yuppie dads cut their allowance by twenty-five bucks for the week as a little negative reinforcement. Whatever it was, they came out and kicked our butts. The first-line center, who I dismissed as a dweeb because he wore number 99 (guys who wear the weird numbers of great players *are* dweebs, even if they can play), beat me for a natural hat trick in the first five minutes. It wasn't rebounds either—just snappy shots that were always a little lower or higher or faster than I thought. Couldn't figure the guy out. My bad.

Of course, there were *also* plenty of uncleared rebounds, three two-on-ones, and one three-on-nothing (Woodsie would have at least made it a three-on-one, but he lost an edge and fell down at the blue line). The whole team—did I call them spoiled yuppies?—played very rough, too, and they clonked us all over the place. Woodsie, who is skinny, spent more time on his pants than on his skates. Cody, who is extremely small, kept racing down the wing with the puck until the defenseman backskating with him would get tired of watching and flick him onto his butt with one hand. It is true that Barry got in a perfect hipcheck on 99 in the second period and 99 did a flip and landed funny and never made it back, but he had done his damage by then anyway. Somebody slashed Shinny and he had to leave to get his wrist X-rayed. Later we found out it was fractured.

Prince finally scored in the third period to give our parents something to clap for, but the whole thing was pitiful. My brother Scott was there, and he would have been pleased, because the whole time I undressed I did nothing but think.

I thought about how Kenny and his new teammates had taken this Reston team to pieces.

I thought about what it must be like to be really talented, as an individual.

I thought about what it must be like to be surrounded by other talented individuals, and be coached by someone who knew how to make you into a team.

I thought, on the other hand, about what it must be like to be really talented and play with a bunch of suckers.

I thought about how I'd always believed last year's Wings were all-round perfect, full of balance and the kind of interaction and special feeling nobody with any sense or loyalty or conscience would mess up.

It is true that last year our team record was fabulous. But—I now realized—it was also true that Kenny Moseby had scored more than half our goals. And the more plays I recalled from big games, the more I remembered it had been *him* poking a puck at center to stop an odd-man rush late in a one-goal game, it had been *him* sliding down to block a slapshot from the circle that would have beat me because I was down on the other side of the net, *him* hustling back and catching a guy on a breakaway and chopping the puck off his stick and turning it back up ice, skating through everyone and flicking it through the goalie's pads to break a tie in the Silver Skates quarterfinal. *Him* double-shifting and playing defense at the end of every close game.

And *him* always, *always* being the first guy to reach me after a game and rub my head and say "Great stops, Zip," before scooting up to start the handshaking.

Jeez. I had to face it: Almost everything last year was Kenny. It's true the four guys who left for Montrose with him were all pretty good too, but even if we had them back we would still be losing—by four goals a game, maybe, instead of by twelve. So what.

For the first time, I got the idea that maybe last year Kenny was off by himself more than we knew, and the rest of us were the "team." He was so humble and nice, nobody would have noticed if he felt lonesome or cranky at being depended on too much. In tight moments when someone was stuck, he'd tap his stick for the puck, and whoever had it would gladly sling it his way, and K would gather it in and off he'd go to save the day.

At least six other guys on last year's team—including the four who followed him to Montrose—had talked loudly at one time or another of being the best player on the team. I remember thinking, "Hey, what games have *you* guys been watching?" But I didn't actually *say* anything.

Of course, Kenny never said anything either. He just went out and scored five or six goals and made eight or nine key defensive plays covering for other guys and skated almost twice as many shifts as some players, and every time he took his helmet off at the end of the game he was grinning and looked like he could do it all over again.

This year, it's me who's off by himself, lonesome *and* cranky, and everybody knows it. But not because I'm so talented. Not because I'm depended on too much.

What exactly is my problem, anyway?

Cody breaks up my profound thinking. "Those guys didn't look half so big last week when we saw them from the luxury box, huh?"

"No. They looked pathetic."

"Yeah, well." Cody stuffs an elbow pad into his bag. "Like my English teacher says, 'Context is everything.'"

I look at him. "Tell me something. Do you know when we get our first encounter with the particular context that Reston found so hostile last week?"

"You mean when do we play the Montrose A's?" Cody wrinkles his forehead at me. "What's with you? You don't read the schedule?"

"I never read the teams on schedules." I blush a little. "I'm superstitious. I don't really want to think about who will be shooting the puck; I, like, pretend my only enemy is the puck itself, and it's the same puck for the whole season and it has nothing to do with people. Sounds weird, I know. So, on the schedule, I just look at the times and show up."

"Well, are you sure you want to know about when we play the Bears, then? Because they, like, have definite personalities, if you know what I mean."

I swallow. "I know what you mean. Sure. Tell me."

"Then how about Wednesday night?"

"*This* Wednesday night?"

"Yup."

My bowels go cold. "They'll score forty goals on me."

"Nah." He zips his bag. "They'll let up after

twenty-five or so—you know that."

He's almost ready to go, but I put out a hand and stop him from getting up. "Cody."

"What?"

"Do I suck?"

He looks at me. "As a person? Or as a goalie?"

"As a goalie."

He rubbed his chin. "Let's just say you used to seem a little quicker. And like maybe you concentrated more. And cared a little more too. You used to *hate* being scored on, but you never yelled at anyone for screwing up in front of you, and it kind of charged everybody up. Everybody kind of wanted to protect you, you know? We sort of thought of you as a leader back there." He shrugs. "So, I don't know, I guess I'd have to say that, you know, because of attitude or whatever, yes, you *do* suck a little bit now. Of course, everyone else sucks at least as much, each in his own special way." He held out his arms to indicate all the guys getting dressed. "Not a man among us free from sin," he said in the voice of a TV minister, "but, ah, we've got the holy spirit."

"You actually do, don't you? Have spirit?"

He looks at me funny. "What's this 'you' stuff? Why not 'we'?"

I throw a skate into my bag. "I guess I feel like I've been kind of holding myself apart."

"Oh, sure, def. You've been a real jerk about it. But it doesn't matter—you *are* on this team and there's nothing anyone can do about it. We're stuck with you, just like you're stuck with us." He gives my bag a little kick. "Hey, it's only you who've been believing you could get a divorce. The rest of us— well, you're just included, that's all." He stands up with his bag and slaps me on the shoulder with mock friendliness. "So be a jerk if you insist, but why not give it up? It's still just playing hockey, isn't it? And who knows—maybe one day we won't lose one." Then he leaves.

And I still sit there thinking. Mostly, all of a sudden, about Wednesday night.

'm doing my report on Alexander freaking Graham Bell Monday night when my mother knocks on my door and says there's a call for me. I gladly get up and go downstairs.

I pick up the receiver. "Kenny?"

Two boys laugh on the other end. "'Kenny, darling?'" one of them says in falsetto. "'Sweetie, remember what pals we are, so don't go and do anything unfriendly, like shoot on me too hard or anything, okay?'" They both laugh again. They sound a little familiar.

"Who is this?" I ask. "Is that you, Pelletier?"

"It's the monsters from your nightmares, goalie. We just want to wish you some sweet dreams for the next couple of nights."

"It *is* you. And who's with you? Moore? You guys are really sick."

"But mostly, we want to reassure you."

"Yeah. We want to let you know we've decided as a team to kind of break you in gently Wednesday night."

"Anything less would be unkind."

"Yeah. Downright unfriendly." They laugh.

"I don't need any breaks from you buttwipes," I say.

"Ah, but we like to make our gestures of good sportsmanship anyway. So guess what? You will be stopping our first five shots Wednesday night. Guaranteed. Absolutely a lock. So, see, you can take the ice and just relax."

"For a while."

"But let's not look ahead—we don't want to alarm him, do we? Five whole shots you don't have to worry about. Just leave everything to us! The thing is, you'll be stopping all five of those shots—bang bang bang bang bang—with your melon. Five shots, right to the head, Zipperoo."

They laugh. I say, "You guys have a pretty outrageous idea of your accuracy."

"Well, Zip, we practice a lot." They howl.

"Come at me, then," I say, trying to sound rough. "Just don't be too disappointed if the shots you take *after* the first five also manage to hit me somewhere."

"Oh, some of them will." Pelletier laughs. "We couldn't resist a couple slappers at the ol' cup. But don't worry—we'll surprise you with those. The rest of them—what did we put on goal against Reston, Jeff, like fifty-one?—the rest will miss you altogether."

"That's a relief," I say. "Otherwise I'd be real scared."

"Well, we're considerate guys."

"Yeah. We got Kenny's feelings to think about." They laugh.

"'Please don't hurt him, boys! He's my old buddy!'" says Moore in falsetto.

"Kenny never asked you anything like that," I say. "He didn't."

"'Zip's really a very sensitive person, so please let's not do anything to damage his self-esteem. I *care* for the boy.'"

"You lie," I say.

They howl together, try to say something more, and can't stop laughing. I hang up.

Thank you, Alexander Graham Bell.

fourteen

I decide not to say anything to Kenny about the call, so I make sure to stay away from him at school the next day. But for some reason he tries especially hard to talk to me, jogging toward me about ten times in the hall and once even following me into the science lab saying, "Zip, please, we got to talk!" but I blow him off every time. I stay after school in the library and stand by a window, watching him wait for me by the front door. He waits forty minutes, then finally leaves. I leave ten minutes later, and take a weird route home.

I drop my books and tell Scott I'm going out until dinner. Then I head for the forest that's still standing on the edge of our housing development, and walk in the woods for about four hours until it's good and dark.

I'm late for dinner and that gets me in trouble and my mother confines me to my room with no

TV, music, or phone calls. After I shut the door I pump my fist and say, *"Yesss!"* Who knows what Montrose players might be calling tonight. Well, they won't reach me.

I'm lying on my bed reading this biography of Nirvana and wondering what in the world could ever make anyone want to take as many drugs as that Cobain guy did, much less blow your head off *really*, when my mother knocks and opens the door. I put the book down and smile, thinking she's come to release me in time for a boring National Geographic special on TV or something.

But she isn't smiling. "Zip," she says, "have you seen Kenny today?"

"Sure. He was at school."

She nods, frowning. "And after school? You didn't spend any of that time with him, when you were gone so long?"

"No. I was alone." I get a little chill between my shoulder blades. "Why? What's happened?"

She looks at me a minute. "Well, he hasn't come home. Marie is on the phone. She's very worried. Apparently Kenny—well, he hasn't been very happy lately, I guess, and he's been acting kind of low and withdrawn. She's afraid—oh, I don't know. She's just afraid he's run away or done something."

I stand up. "Let me talk to her."

She steps aside and I go down to the phone.

"Mrs. Moze? It's Zip."

"Zip! Oh, Zip! Have you heard from Kenny? I know he must have come to see you; you're practically all he—"

"Is his hockey bag there?"

She stops talking. "His . . . ? I—well, I don't know. I mean, I suppose it is. He doesn't have anything until tomorrow night's game, so there's no reason—"

"Just go check."

"All right. Hold on." She puts down the phone and I hear her footsteps going quickly away. In a minute they come quickly back.

"Zip, it's gone. He keeps it in the corner of his room and it's—"

"Listen, Mrs. Moseby. Why don't you swing by and pick me up? I think we can find Kenny pretty easy. And he's okay."

"What—where—"

"Just come pick me up, okay?"

"Well—all right. All right, Zip. If you know—"

"I'll be out front."

I hang up, run up the stairs past my mother coming down, go into my room, get something from the bottom drawer of my bureau, and start back for the stairs. But then I stop, and think. And go back and get my own hockey stuff.

My mother's at the foot of the stairs. "Zip, what on earth—"

"Finding Kenny," I say, opening the front door. "It's okay. Be back late." I close it and run down the front walk.

Thirty seconds later Mrs. Moseby's Bronco pulls up. I open the back and throw my stuff in, then climb in next to her in front. She looks at me with an expression exactly halfway between fear and curiosity. "Why did you bring your pads? Is Kenny at a rink?"

"I'm betting he is. But not one you know about."

I give her directions. We go way out of town, down some dark roads, past some abandoned small factories, across a railyard.

"Did Kenny *walk* here?" she asks. "With his hockey bag?"

"Unless he hitched."

She shudders, and makes the last turn I'd told her to make. And there we are. In a small parking lot of broken asphalt and dirt, facing a big rusty quonset hut.

"Is that—"

"We found it that time we 'ran away' for almost a whole day when we were about seven," I tell her. "Remember you had to come almost to Marshfield to pick us up? It belongs to the company that used to own one of those factories back there. The guy who started the company was from Canada and he built it so his employees could play hockey after work. We found all this out from a guy; there was a game of old dudes going on when we discovered it. It's still used for pick-up leagues, but not much, because it's too small a sheet." I look at her. "I'm going to get my stuff on. You got to wait here."

"No way, Zip! If Kenny is in that place—"

I touch her arm. She shuts up. "Just let me, okay? Things are messed up between Kenny and me, and maybe that's even one reason he's run away. So let me try something, all right?"

She looks at me. She shakes her head. But she says, "All right."

I hop out and go around back and get out my stuff and quickly put it on. I wait to put on my skates until I've walked across the cracked parking lot to one of the three doors with loose latches Kenny and I found the second time we came here. Then I put on my skates, take a few deep breaths, jiggle the lock just right, and open the door. There's darkness inside—this is a locker room—but under the door over on the other side of the room I see a line of light.

I go in and close the door quietly. I walk across the room, and pause by the door to take off my skate guards. From the other side, off in the distance, I hear the *thwack* of a hockey stick hitting a hockey puck. Then I open the door and step out into a small tunnel that leads to the gate onto the ice. The place is suddenly silent.

Without looking, I open the gate, step onto the ice, close the gate, turn, skate toward the nearest cage, spin into position, and finally look up.

There he is, standing straight up at center ice under one of the old hanging bulb lights, his stick in one hand, a puck at his feet. He isn't wearing his helmet, and I can see from his eyes that he's been crying or something.

He's wearing his old Wings jersey.

"Wrong shirt, Kenny," I say.

He looks down at his chest. "Zip," he says, "I'm so sorry, I'm just so sorry. I never—"

"Do you have your Bears shirt in your bag?"

He blinks for a second, then nods.

"Then don't be a wuss. Go put it on, then come back, and let me stone your sorry ass."

He blinks again, but he gives a little smile. Then he skates to a gate at the far end, goes out, and comes back a minute later wearing his blue Montrose road jersey.

"Warm me up," I tell him.

He skates down to about ten feet away and looks up. I nod. He lifts a soft wrist shot that I hit with my blocker. Then he gets the puck, comes back, and does it again and again, about thirty times, the shots getting a little harder and a little tougher to reach as he goes.

Finally I'm warm and I say, "Okay. Let's do it."

"What?" he asks. "Listen, Zip, I—"

"Shut up. We are going to do a scientific experiment. A geometric proof. An objective demonstration." I look at him. "A clearing of anger and guilt."

"What do you imagine could do *that*?"

"You are going to skate around and shoot on me and I am going to try to stop you. And you are going to shoot your best. Maybe you won't at first, because you're still feeling a little guilty, but you'll get the hang of it, and your hockey self will take over. I know you. You'll try to beat me, slappers, wrist shots close in, bad angles, every hot thing you can think of. And I promise you"—I point my stick at him—"I'm going to keep everything out of this net that I can."

He watches me as I set myself in position. "So what's all this supposed to prove?"

"That we've both been weenies, but especially me. Come on! Shoot the puck, Moseby!"

Without moving, he snaps a wrister low to the left corner. I sprawl my skate out and knock it to the corner. "That blew," I say. "But you'll do better."

He skates over, gathers the puck, looks at me, shakes his head, and starts skating around the top of the circle. As soon as he reaches the curve toward the slot, without looking up he launches a looping backhander that sails right over my shoulder and in.

"Nice," I say. "You let it go a little early."

He shrugs. "Been working on stuff like that. Some no-look shots, a little surprise timing."

I shoot the puck back at him. "More."

And he starts to get into it, skating harder, shooting harder, moving farther away and coming at me from every angle, sometimes deking around an imaginary defenseman, sometimes stopping suddenly to let one whiz by, sometimes tapping the puck to one side of an imagined opponent and twirling around him in a tight spin to pick it up on the other side and shoot. He gradually shows some moves I know he had only thought about: stops and starts, tight curls with the puck on his backhand, dekes with one shoulder, both shoulders, just his head, or one knee. He moves out to the blue line and takes twenty slapshots, putting English on them so they curve, rise, or drop. He goes all the way to the other end, skates full speed up the wing to a foot short of the goal line, and fires a curving shot from the corner off his back skate. I'm holding the post but it goes in around me. At some point his mom had come in to watch from the shadows, and I hear her gasp at that one.

After about half an hour he's dead tired and so am I, so I kick out one last backhand he'd taken from a bad angle and hold up my glove. "Enough," I pant. I pull off my mask. He skeets to a stop, and spins to face me.

His eyes don't look like they had been crying anymore. They look like the eyes I saw once in a picture of a peregrine falcon. The brown hair on his forehead is slick with sweat. His cheeks look like somebody had painted dark pink circles neatly on them. He isn't smiling, but only because he isn't sure he's supposed to. This is Kenny Moseby, happy hockey boy.

"You look pretty good," I say.

"Thanks. So do you," he says.

"Thanks. I thought I made some pretty good saves."

"You did," he says. "That one when I spun and looked high and shot low, that was—"

"Do you know how many saves I made?"

He wrinkles his forehead. "What do you mean?"

"I counted," I say. "I told you. This is a scientific experiment. Quantitatively measured."

"What—"

"You took a hundred and sixty-one shots on me, including that half-ass backhander at the end. And I made precisely seventeen saves. Including the half-ass backhander."

He shrugs. "So? Like you said, some of them were—"

I hold up my glove. "Think about it. I mean, it's a fair test, I think. You shot, a hundred and sixty-one times. I did my best to stop you, and I did, seventeen times." I put my glove down and stared him in the eye. He starts to look uncomfortable. "Now: Do we belong on the same team?"

"Zip, listen—"

"It's not you who needs to face the answer, Kenny. It's me. I'm sorry. I'm really sorry. All along I couldn't decide if it was hockey or me, and I wasn't thinking very clear about myself either way." I skate over a couple of feet. He looks up at me. "Sorry, Kenny. You did the right thing. I've sucked as a friend."

He shaves some ice with his skates, looking

down. "I came out here tonight, I was thinking about quitting."

"I figured it might be something like that."

"I don't have any friends on the team. I mean, we win and stuff, but those guys just—"

"You don't have to have friends on every hockey team you play on. Hockey teams are for playing hockey."

"Yeah, but the Wings—"

"We're nice guys. And we're 0-9-0, and it sucks to lose that bad. So you can't do it on friendship alone, either." I wait until he looks up at me. "Play normal tomorrow night, okay? We will, that's for sure. It's just another game." I kick the puck toward center ice. "And we'll do one penalty shot for who buys the pizza after."

He dekes backhand and goes forehand. They almost always do. I stop him.

fifteen

Before the game I stand up in the locker room and call for quiet.

"This will be a short speech," I say. "I apologize for what a jerk I've been."

"You can't help it," says Barry.

"Yeah," says Dooby, "you were born that way, and you'll die that way."

"Maybe tonight," says Cody.

Shinny, who's in street clothes with his hand in a cast, says, "There is, of course, only one instance of a player actually—"

"Shut up, Shinny. Just because you got hurt doesn't mean you're suddenly not boring."

"How many shots do these guys average per game?" asks Barry.

"An inside source told me they put fifty-one on Reston," I say.

"So are you ready for that, Marshall?"

Marshall, who's putting on his skates, looks up in horror. "Me? I'm not—"

"Didn't Coach tell you? Zip strained his back."

"I thought—I mean, these guys—usually, Coach puts me in against, you know—"

Everybody roars. "The Sniper poops his pants," Prince says.

"I'm not afraid of anyone," Marshall says.

"Not much."

"Relax, Marshall," I say. "I *want* these guys."

"The return of the Real Zip," Dooby says.

"We *all* want these guys," says Barry. "Right, Boot?"

"The Boot welcomes all challenges."

"Then get a hat trick on Cheerios," Barry tells him.

"If you can get to him through the defense. I hear it's awesome."

"Anybody actually watched them this year?"

"Yeah," says Cody. Everybody looks at him. "Zip and I saw them play." They wait. He shrugs. "The Canadiens kicked their *tails*."

"But it was in Montreal," I put in. "They'll be tougher here."

"No, really," says Ernie. "What are they like?"

Coach Cooper walks in just then and takes over. "They're all very nice boys who respect their mothers," he says. "They don't eat meat or wear any animal products, they kneel to pray before every face-off, and if one of them curses on the ice he vanishes in a puff of smoke and goes straight to the Bad Place Opposite of Heaven."

"Are they going to kill us?" asks Ernie.

"Frankly, yes," says Coach Coop. "Unless we do a few things right. First of all, hit every one of them every chance you get, and hit them low. They're bigger than we are, so if you shoulder-check them, you're going down. But they are not used to getting hit. Pop 'em at the hips."

"That sounds disturbing," says Dooby, covering his ears.

"Also, don't hesitate to put your stick on the puck anytime it comes past you headed in the wrong direction. You guys are all so clean about carrying and passing and covering. Today if you see the puck, jab it, even if you haven't got a clear pass in mind. They run a lot of set plays and the slightest poke can mess them up." He looks around. "Billy."

Billy is in the corner where his dad, as usual, is getting him dressed. They both look at the Coach.

"Billy, I want you to take one for the team today. I want you to fight Number 27, Pelletier, probably sometime in the second period. You don't have to kill him or even win, just make sure you both get your gloves off and swing a lot. Of course, if you can, kick his butt, but it isn't necessary."

Billy gulps and looks down at his dad. Billy is the youngest kid on the team and talks the most violent. He also has the worst temper. His dad is a big guy who used to play college football and seems very concerned about toughness. He says to the Coach, "Won't that get him suspended?"

"One game," says Coach Coop. "Saturday morning. He'll be playing again Saturday afternoon. What do you say, Billy?"

Everybody watches him look at his dad, who gives a twitch of the mouth that must have signified approval. Billy smiles. "I'll break his nose."

"That will be hard through his face shield, so just try to engage him in a pretty harmless battle. Thank you. I'll tell you when. Now, one more thing." He holds up his hand. There is silence.

"We all know this team now features several players who used to be teammates of many of you here at Wolfbay. Certainly I understand that there has been resentment built up about this, a good deal of anger and feelings of betrayal. Am I right, Doobs?"

"I have no idea what you're talking about." Everyone laughs.

"Well, if you think I want to sit on the bench and watch you take out your personal frustrations on those players and their new teammates, if you think I am going to allow you to lose your cool and let yourselves be motivated by spite and revenge, if you think I'm going to watch silently while you throw your energy into really punishing anyone in a blue sweater because of your petty inability to wish your old teammates well, then you are absolutely right. The only way we are going to stay on the ice with these guys is if we are motivated. Stay smart, play clean, but be terribly, terribly angry."

There's a huge cheer and then I lead us out of the locker room and onto the ice.

I notice there's an unusually large crowd for the game, but that figures: The departure of the club's superstar and other good players has been a big issue among the adults as well as the kids. But I don't hear the crowd or anything. For the first time all year, I lock into what I used to call Goalie Magic. It's a state of consciousness I had forgotten about but used to find myself in for every game, in which I heard no words, had no thoughts, focused on no individuals. I just watched the puck. . . .

I don't remember a single moment of warm-ups. I don't remember skating to the bench and hearing Coach set the lines and give a pep talk. I don't remember chanting *"Let's fly, Wings!"* like we always do before taking the ice. I just remember being in the pipes and waiting for the puck to be dropped.

Once the game started, I was nothing but reflexes. One parent later told me it was the smartest game he'd ever seen a goalie play and that's a real hoot, because I never had an idea for the entire time. I do not remember much. I remember that, as promised, the Bears' shooters hit me in the mask with three of their first four shots, until the ref saw what was up and warned them. I didn't care. I do remember my defensemen shouting a lot to each other, and I remember seeing the puck swept out from in front of me after a lot of rebounds, which means I made a lot of saves. I remember letting in a goal on a deflection, and another on a slapshot from the point that I almost caught, but it was so hard it ripped through my glove. I remember cheers from the other end a couple of times.

When the period changed I didn't go to the bench but just skated down to the other cage. I passed Cheerios on the way but we didn't speak.

The second period, I remember, was more of the same—lots of skates around my face and sticks crossing in my crease and pucks suddenly flying at me and hitting some part of my body. Apparently at some point Billy did fight Pelletier and got his helmet off and belted him a couple of good ones, but I do not recall it at all.

Period over. Skate back down to the other cage. Face-off. More seeing the puck dart here and there between sticks, then off a skate, then back to a stick, and then a thud against my shin and the puck goes away. I remember noticing at one point that Woodsie and Barry and Dooby, all defensemen near enough that I saw their faces, looked incredibly intense and alert and happy. I remember once someone was coming in on a breakaway and drew his stick back for a slapper from the high slot, but before he could swing, the puck came at me slow and straight on the ice because Woodsie had dived from behind and nudged it to me and I sticked it to the corner.

Finally, I remember the Montrose captain calling their timeout, and everybody but me skating to the benches. That was when I looked at the scoreboard for the first time in the whole game.

It said WINGS 2—VISITORS 2.

Really? I thought to myself. *Were those the only two I let in? Pretty good. And we scored twice? Okay.* I looked back up to see the time. There was 1:33 left.

I wish I hadn't looked. Because as the players came back after the timeout, I realized I was out of the zone. I had broken the Goalie Magic. I was conscious. And it hit me: We could tie this incredible team, maybe even beat them. It was terrible news.

Because from that point on, I was at least partly a thinker, not just a set of reflexes. I had to start "trying" instead of just reacting, and it was much harder. I got very lucky once when I completely missed a shot with my glove and it hit the crossbar and bounced to Cody, who zipped up ice and made some trouble down there in front of Cheerios, using up some time. A defenseman tried to clear, but Barry stopped it and fired a low hard shot and I screamed *"Yesss!"* but Cheerios kicked it out and one of their wingers collected the rebound. For the first time all day I noticed the identity of one of their players, when I recognized, with a sinking feeling, that the kid with the puck was Kenny.

Of course, I thought, as I watched him wheel out of the zone and weave through our lunging guys at center ice. *Who else could it be?* The seconds were ticking like clicks in my spine as he skeeted to a stop at the blue line to avoid a two-handed slash at the puck by Barry, then started a straight sprint right at me.

"Come on, nosehole!" I hollered like I always do, and I set myself, and all of the moves he had pulled on me last night raced through my head and I made myself focus on him as if we were back once years ago when we were running toward each other from two ends of a big culvert, just Kenny and me alone in a tunnel, alone in the world. Here he

came, the puck on his forehand, his shoulder dipping, my knees dropping—

But the trouble is, we weren't alone in the world, and at the last second Kenny flicked the puck across the crease right beneath my eyes, to his right wing, who had been skating in on me too, completely unseen. All he had to do was put his stick on the ice and I watched Kenny's pass turn into the winning goal.

I was frozen on my knees. A voice above me said, "See what a chump you were for taking it so personal?" and I looked up to see Kenny grinning as he skated away. The winger who scored was mobbed. I never even saw who he was. There was time for the face-off at center, which Prince won, but before we could skate with it the buzzer sounded.

Everyone's coming at me. Ernie gets there first and whoops and leaves his skates completely and knocks me down and people start piling on. I'm screaming at them, calling them all jerks and buttheads and losers, but they're laughing, and jabbing my mask with their gloves, and howling and whopping some more. *"But we lost!"* I keep hollering, but nobody hears me except Prince, who is smiling huge behind his face cage smashed against mine at the bottom of the pile.

"No, baby," Prince says. "They got one more little tiny goal than we did, but we whupped their mighty heinie and they know it."

And he's right. In the handshake line it's us, the Wings, who are smiling and pumping the hands hard, and it's the Bears, the still undefeated Bears, who are gray-faced and gloomy and fish-handed. All those checks and pokes must have taken their toll. This was a team that no longer believed it couldn't lose.

Maybe we were a team that no longer believed it couldn't win.

I'm last in the handshake line, and Kenny has skated back so he'll be last too. His helmet is on, but I can see he has peregrine eyes.

"You were afraid to shoot on me," I say. "You knew I would have stoned your butt."

He laughs. "You were a dope for not anticipating the pass."

"You owe me a pizza," I tell him.

"See you in twenty minutes," he says.

Here's a sneak peek at the next book in the

Wolfbay Wings ice hockey

series by Bruce Brooks

CODY

available from HarperCollins

Me and Zip got a gig.

One Tuesday night I was over in his basement and we were playing. I had found this cool chord—I was thinking it must almost be a real one, because my left fingers looked so stretched, the way left hands played on *Unplugged*. It sounded pretty good too, and all four of my fingers were actually holding the strings down all the way and the two strings left open jangled great against the ones I was pinning down. I was slamming the chord for a while, then Zip said, "Sound it out, man," and slowed his drumming down to a cool slow *boom-boppa-boom* on the floor tom-tom. I slowed down too and did my pick across the strings so you could hear each one separate for a second. It was awesome. Then we speeded up again and I started whanging my pick up fast from the bottom to the top for a change, and that was awesome too.

Then the guy comes in.

He's a high school kid. I see him around some-times, he lives somewhere around here; he's always alone, and I thought he was kind of weird. He has a nose ring and all the hair cut off one side of his head and never wears a coat but only this big flannel shirt with the elbows out, and he wears these green boots he must have bought at an Army store, they're really *green*. He's always reading some thick book while he walks. My brother, who isn't really a nerd himself, has told me about the sci-fi nerds in high school. They are, like, the worst, and I thought maybe this guy was one. So anyway, this kid isn't legally a stranger, but he does open Zip's basement door and just steps in, which, you know, is sort of unusual.

We stop playing and Zip says, "Who the bleep are you?"

"You guys got something going," he says. "I've heard you before when I walk by some nights."

"So?" I say.

He looks at me. "That was a righteous chord you had there."

I can't help feeling a little good, but I just kind

of grunt and twist at a tuning key.

He looks at Zip. "You change speeds great. Sudden. It's . . . confident."

I'm sure Zip has never exactly used that word to describe his whacking at the drums, but instead of laughing he decides to accept it and he actually says, "Thanks."

Then the guy looks at us both and says, "So, do you want a gig?"

"You mean play for people? Somewhere else?"

The kid laughs. "Unless you can talk your parents into hosting a party for fifty kids in their basement here, yes. It would be at the elementary school. The cafeteria has a stage."

"A *school*?" I said.

He looks at me and nods. Then he has to flip his hair back with his hand, and I can tell it's as automatic for him as putting the puck from backhand to forehand is for me. Which means he's had this haircut a long time, which is kind of cool. Other kids are just starting to do halfhead cuts.

"It's, like, a party, all approved and everything. The high school literary magazine holds one every fall when the first issue gets published. The kids are arty-punk types." He looks a little embarrassed. "They're not dweebs or anything, but they're not exactly headbangers."

"And what will they do while we play?" Zip asks. "Sit around and read?"

"Maybe they get naked and paint each other," I say.

"No, sorry," the kid says with a nice laugh. "Some will just hang around and talk, some will goof around and laugh, and some will stand near the stage and listen. A lot will dance."

"*Dance?*" says Zip.

"To *us?*" I say. "*That* sounds nuts."

The kid laughed again.

"I'm just saying I know some kids who I think will really like your music."

"That's even more nuts."

"Yeah. We, like, don't, you know, think this is like *music* or anything. It's just—I don't know—"

"Sound," the kid suggests.

Something about the way he says it makes Zip suspicious. "Yes," he says, in a phony voice like a guidance counselor uses. "The true, spontaneous, uncontrolled sound of the Young Generation. The neo-grunge, the spastic hash of the *real* true totally uncrafted universe of preteens. The new, no-chord, free-beat *trash* sound."

Now the guy really laughs. "I can't deny that probably some kids will actually think that way. I told you—these are not your usual kids. They—well, they are prepared to find art where other people find, um, like, a lack of skill or something."

"They ought to come to some of our hockey games, then," says Zip.

"You play hockey? Cool!"

"Our team sucks, though," says Zip. "So it's not all *that* cool."

"So, what do you say?"

"When's this party?" I ask.

"Next Friday night."

"What time?"

"Starts at ten. Goes until probably two. No alcohol, you can tell your parents. School security guard outside and in, watching the clock and all that. Very cool."

"We can't," I say, but Zip says louder, "What do we get paid?"

The kid smiles. "You mean you won't play for

art's sake?" Then he says, "We can give you four hundred bucks."

I say, "We won't play for *hockey's* sake, unfortunately. We got a game at six A.M. Saturday."

Zip waves me off. "We suck anyway. So what if you and I are a little tired?" He grins at the kid. "We'll play for five hundred."

The kid shakes his head, like he can't believe it. "I'm getting hustled by a twelve-year-old. No, really—we got a budget. Four bills is it."

"Sorry," I say. "It's not the money, right, Zip? It's just we—"

"Deal," Zip says.

"Cool," says the guy. "I'll be in touch." He opens the door, then turns back. "Do you have a band name or something?"

"Yeah," said Zip. "You can call us Puck You Two."

The guy leaves.

"Zip!" I say. "What's your problem?"

He whacks out a sloppy roll on his floor tom. "Come on, Codes. It will be the coolest. Making noise for a bunch of art goofs for serious money!" He laughs. "Let's practice so we stay nice and natural. Wouldn't want to acquire any skills."

"We got a game at six. Against Bowie."

He smacks his snare. "The very same team who just beat Reston 11–1."

"Yeah, I know, and Reston beat us, so that means we'll lose, but you know it doesn't work like that. We're different since the Montrose game. *You're* different."

"Not so different I can't use two hundred dollars," he says. "And the team isn't so different it stands a chance against Bowie, even if we got to bed at *seven* o'clock Friday night." He puts his sticks down and looks at me.

"Seriously, Codes—it's not like we're going to skip the game or something. We'll just stay up late."

"More like all night. Have you ever played a hockey game after staying up all night?"

"Yes!" he says, laughing. "I'm a *goalie*, you moron. Goalies don't sleep before games. I twist and turn and groan and thrash around. Then I give up and get up and go downstairs with my Discman and listen to Bad Brains music until it's time to get psycho."

"That's not the same. You'll be wasted."

"Nah. I'll be *loose*. And, look, you don't exactly

have to work up a sweat at this gig either. You can probably sit on a stool and twang two chords the whole time. If you can learn two chords in ten days."

I put down a couple of fingers and play a loud one. It sounds like someone dropped a tray of food. It's great. I can't help smiling.

"See? You already learned one," says Zip, picking up his sticks and dinging a long line of beats on his big cymbal.

I twang again, but with another finger down. It sounds even raunchier. Zip smashes his cymbal and it's like a car getting hit. "We *are* the best," I say.

"We're a *band*." He does a little press roll on his snare, or what passes for a press roll from Zip. "Hey. Cody." I look at him. He grins and says, "Puck you."

I smile back. Maybe it would be okay. "Puck You *Two*," I say.

"And who knows?" he says. "Maybe we'll be so chilled we'll beat Bowie."